Rudy Visits the North

FIRST U.S. EDITION
10 9 8 7 6 5 4 3 2 1

ISBN: 1-56282-182-2 (trade)
ISBN: 1-56282-208-X (lib. bdg.)

Library of Congress Catalogue Card Number: 91-75423

Book design by A. O. Osen
The artwork for each picture is prepared with acrylics.
This book is set in 14-point Palatino.

THE ADVENTURES OF RUDY BEAR

Rudy Visits the North

Story by Aubrey Lang

Illustrations by Muriel Hope

Hyperion Books for Children

One day in late September, a little black bear was sitting under his favorite scratching tree in the Pennsylvania forest where he lived. His name was Rudy. He was enjoying his first summer on his own and he had spent his time romping through the woods looking for acorns and beechnuts, and chasing mice and frogs and woodchucks. Now that the leaves were falling he should have been looking for a winter den, but he wasn't anxious to go to sleep.

"It's so boring being in a den," he announced. "Playing is much more fun."

The more Rudy thought about sleeping the more determined he was to stay awake.

"I'd like to have an adventure," he said. "Perhaps I could travel to some faraway place."

The other residents of the forest were somewhat surprised at Rudy's strange behavior over the next few weeks. He was scurrying around the forest gathering acorns and berries, and stuffing them into a backpack made out of bark.

"Bears don't gather food," they said. "Why do you need to store food in a backpack?"

"I'm going on a trip," answered Rudy, "to visit my polar bear cousins near Hudson Bay."

"Are you going to the North for the winter?" asked the owl in his serious voice.

"Yes I am," answered Rudy, "for an adventure."

"You really shouldn't go," advised the owl. "It's much too cold."

"And too far," chirped the redpoll.

"What will you eat?" continued the worried owl. "You can't find food in the ice and snow."

"Look," said the little bear showing them his backpack. "I've been collecting nuts and berries to take with me. I'm sure I have all the food I'll need."

Rudy set out immediately. He walked for three weeks. His feet were sore, and the map he had brought along was torn and crumpled from using it so much. "Will it ever stop snowing?" he asked wearily, as he tried to push through the white drifts. "I'm so tired. The snow is too deep for my short legs. How will I ever get to Hudson Bay to see my cousins?" Tears filled his eyes and froze in little drops on his long nose. Discouraged, he sank into the snow to rest. Soon a fluffy white blanket covered him and he settled into a deep sleep.

Rudy was awakened by several sharp blows on his head. "Ouch," he yelled, jumping up from the snow and smacking his lips to show how angry he was. He stared with defiance at a strange animal that stood high above the snow on long skinny legs. Clouds of steam came out of the animal's big nose as he snorted and tossed his head. He looked fierce.

"Oh!" cried Rudy, shaking with fright, "This is the end of me!" As the big animal started towards him, Rudy tried to escape, but he only sank deeper into the snow.

"Where are you going?" asked the stranger in a rumbling voice. "There is no need to run away, I don't eat bears."

"I'm sorry I hit you on the head, but I was pawing through the snow looking for something to eat. My name is Moose. Who are you?"

Rudy was still afraid, but he tried to be brave.

"My name is Rudy, and I'm going north to visit my cousins. Do you know how far it is to Hudson Bay?"

The big moose looked thoughtful. "I'd like to help you," he said, "but that is too far for me to go and the snow is too deep for you to walk."

Rudy was very disappointed, but he couldn't think of going home. He had to find a way to get to Hudson Bay.

Suddenly Moose interrupted his thoughts. "There's a train that goes there," he announced. "I'll guide you to the tracks, but you must climb on my back so I can get you through these drifts."

Moose had a broad back covered with thick fur, but it was slippery from the wet snow. Rudy tried to balance, but he kept sliding to one side and then the other as the big animal lumbered through the trees.

Fearful that he would fall, Rudy used his long sharp claws to get a better grip. Immediately Moose began to jump and twist, and Rudy was tossed head first into the snow.

As he landed he heard a loud crack. One of Moose's antlers had struck a low branch and snapped off. When Rudy looked up he saw that Moose had lost part of his head.

"Will you die?" Rudy asked, fearfully. He stared in amazement at the antler lying beside him and then at his lop-sided friend.

"Don't worry," Moose reassured him, "my antlers always fall off in the winter. We can use this one to make a toboggan to get you to the train."

"What fun this is," said Rudy as the big animal glided through the drifts pulling the bear behind him.

In the distance Rudy could see a cloud of smoke and he heard a deep roar. He had never seen a train before and he wondered how he would ride it. "Could you come with me on this train?" he asked, somewhat fearfully.

"No, little bear," Moose replied. "I live here and I don't want to leave. If you are going to visit your cousins you must get on the train by yourself."

"How do I get on?" asked Rudy.

"Climb that tree over there," Moose said. "Hurry!"

Rudy climbed the tree and watched the train approaching. It looked like a big snake winding through the snow and Rudy watched it with some fascination. He moved farther along the limb and as it bent under his weight, he found himself hanging upside down directly over the railway tracks. The black engine blew smoke and clanged its bell as it passed underneath Rudy.

"Jump," yelled Moose. "Jump now."

Rudy let go of the branch and landed with a thud on top of the train.

As the little bear hung on tightly he shouted to Moose. "Goodbye," he said, and the wind carried the echoes of his voice around him. He sat stiffly on top of the boxcar, afraid to look back.

The train rolled on and Rudy surveyed the surrounding countryside. He could see for miles and miles. The northern forest was not at all like his forest back home. The trees were shorter and they had needles instead of leaves. The farther north the train went, the fewer trees there were. Soon there were hardly any trees at all and everything was white.

When the train finally stopped, Rudy looked around at the unfamiliar surroundings. It was snowing so hard that he couldn't see a thing and he had no idea how he would find his cousins in the blizzard. He mustered up all of his courage and climbed off the boxcar and began to walk.

He was thinking about what he should do when three
ghostly shapes appeared in front of him. It was Meetuk,
Tuktuk, and Aunt Koo who had moved inland towards the
town to look for food.

"Am I glad to see you," Rudy said as the bears touched
noses and exchanged friendly bites.

His cousins were about the same age as Rudy, but they were bigger and stronger, and they kept knocking him over with their playful shoves. When they smelled Rudy's backpack they immediately sampled the unusual food. Once they started, they ate everything in sight, even the honeycomb that Rudy was saving for a treat.

Aunt Koo sighed and looked at Rudy's sad face. "From now on you'll have to live as polar bears do," she told him.

The next morning the three young bears chased each other across the ice in a game of tag, but Rudy kept slipping and falling. One time Meetuk ran towards the open water of the Bay. When she reached the edge of the water she quickly swerved, but Rudy, who was following close behind, couldn't stop on the ice and slid straight into the frigid water. Meetuk and Tuktuk laughed and jumped into the Bay to swim and play with their cousin. When they all climbed back onto the ice they shook the water from their fur and went to find Aunt Koo.

"How come you never slip and fall on the ice?" Rudy asked his cousins.

"Have a look," said Meetuk as she rolled on her back and waved her feet in the air.

Rudy stared at the rough pads and the fur on her feet and then looked at his own feet. "I wish I had rough pads too, and a little more fur," he said. "My feet are always cold and I can't walk on the ice without sliding."

In the weeks that followed, Aunt Koo and the three young bears wandered along the shore of Hudson Bay. The weather was cold and clear and Aunt Koo frequently stopped to sniff the air. She was waiting for the water in the Bay to freeze so that she could go out onto the ice to hunt seals. While she was waiting the family explored the Tundra and showed Rudy many new things.

"Come on Rudy," said Tuktuk as he bounded in front of his cousin towards a tall snowdrift. "Watch me!" he shouted, and he dived head first off the drift and slid down the slope on his belly.

"Oh, let me try," said Rudy. "This is so much fun," he said. "I've never been sliding before. You certainly can have a good time when you don't have to sleep all winter."

Aunt Koo and Meetuk watched from a distance. They were gathering moss and bark to make a surprise for Rudy. "Black bears are not common in the North," Aunt Koo said. "We must try to make Rudy comfortable while he is here."

Finally the weather turned very cold. Hudson Bay froze and Aunt Koo moved the family onto the ice to hunt for seals. After days of walking, Rudy's feet hurt. There were huge blocks of broken ice with sharp edges, and sometimes the ice was stacked as high as a house. The ice was always moving, cracking, and splitting, and it made weird groaning noises that made Rudy nervous.

One day Aunt Koo suddenly stopped in her tracks. She sniffed the wind. Meetuk and Tuktuk stopped as well and lifted their noses into the air, copying their mother. They had caught the scent of a seal! Rudy sniffed too, but he didn't smell anything that he recognized.

Aunt Koo decided that she would stalk the seal alone.
The three young bears hid behind a piece of ice to watch.
Rudy tried to concentrate on what his aunt was doing,
but he was tired and he quickly fell asleep.

The seal was lying on the ice next to its breathing hole
that led to the water below. It was wary, ready to dive if it
sensed any danger. Aunt Koo was an expert hunter and
she knew all the tricks. When she crept forward, she was
careful not to scratch the ice with her claws, and she
crawled on her belly staying as flat as she could so the seal
wouldn't see her.

Inch by inch, Aunt Koo moved towards the seal, but just as she was about to jump, the ice shifted and cracked. It made a loud bang that sounded like a firecracker. The noise woke Rudy and it scared him so much that he rushed towards his aunt for safety. In the confusion the seal dived into its hole and was gone.

The next day there was a blizzard. The wind blew so fiercely that Rudy had to hold onto his aunt's tail to keep from getting lost in the whiteout. Aunt Koo led them across a treacherous ice fence and headed for a huge snowdrift. Here she dug a snow cave to get the family out of the storm. Rudy was surprised that it was so warm inside the cave. He wondered if the winters were as cold as this back in Pennsylvania and he suddenly felt homesick. He was hungry too, and the wind had chilled his big ears.

"Don't worry," Meetuk told him, "the storm won't last. Besides, Mother has thought of a way to help you."

"We have a surprise," said Tuktuk and he handed Rudy earmuffs made of reindeer moss.

Meetuk gave Rudy some shoes made out of bark. "The bark is rough and the shoes will keep you from slipping on the ice," she explained.

"And the earmuffs will keep your big ears warm," added Tuktuk.

"What great gifts," said Rudy. The thoughtfulness of his aunt and cousins cheered him up. When the storm passed the bears left the snow cave, and that night Rudy wore his new shoes and earmuffs and went to sleep on the edge of the ice.

The next morning, Meetuk and Tuktuk woke up early, but Rudy was nowhere in sight. They thought he was hiding, but no matter where they looked they couldn't find him. They called Aunt Koo and she swam out among the ice floes to look for the little black bear.

"Rudy is lost," she said. "We must find him. He can't survive by himself in the North."

When Rudy woke up, he was far away from his aunt and cousins. The ice he had fallen asleep on had broken off during the night and floated away, but he didn't hear it because he was wearing his earmuffs.

"Where am I?" shouted Rudy. "Aunt Koo! Aunt Koo!" he cried, but no one heard him. "I've got to find my way back," he said and he jumped into the water and began to swim.

Without warning, three large beluga whales surfaced near Rudy. He was so terrified that he scrambled back onto the ice floe and stared at the huge creatures.

The whales circled the ice floe and blew steam from the holes in their backs. They were curious about Rudy and they wanted to play, but Rudy was too afraid to speak to them. The whales rocked the ice floe, but when Rudy didn't respond one of the whales came closer.

"You're a strange-colored bear," the whale observed. "I thought you were a seal."

"No," stammered Rudy, who had finally found his voice. "I come from the South. There are lots of black bears there."

"Well little black bear, you are a long way from the South now," continued the whale. "What are you doing on this ice floe?"

"I'm lost," replied Rudy, "and I want to go home. I've had enough adventure."

"I'm sure we can help you," said the whale and he began to push the ice floe with his great white nose.

It wasn't long before the ice floes began to jam together. "You can walk to shore now," the whale said as he and the other whales headed back towards the sea. "I hope you find your way home."

The wind blew the snow in swirls around Rudy as he climbed over the big mounds of ice. He realized that he had lost his shoes and his earmuffs. "It's not that I don't like the North," Rudy said to himself. "There's lots of exciting things to do here, but I don't seem to be suited to this place."

"Is that you, Rudy Bear?" squawked an old raven sitting on a telephone pole. "Your aunt asked me to look for you. If you want to get on the train I can lead you to the station."

Rudy thanked the raven. He knew he would miss his aunt and cousins but he wanted to be back in his own forest. When he reached the station he climbed on top of the boxcar and stood up to wave to the raven. "Goodbye," he called. "I had a great time."